THE ALIEN ADVENTURES OF FINN CASPIAN

JOURNEY TO THE CENTER OF THAT THING

Read more of Finn Caspian's alien adventures!

THE ALIEN ADVENTURES OF FINN CASPIAN

JOURNEY TO THE CENTER OF THAT THING

Jonathan Messinger

Illustrated by Aleksei Bitskoff

HARPER

An Imprint of HarperCollins*Publishers*

The Alien Adventures of Finn Caspian #4: Journey to the Center of That Thing
Text copyright © 2021 by Jonathan Messinger
Illustrations copyright © 2021 by HarperCollins Publishers
Illustrations by Aleksei Bitskoff

Library of Congress Control Number: 2021933142
ISBN 978-0-06-293224-2 — ISBN 978-0-06-293223-5 (pbk.)

Typography by Jessie Gang
21 22 23 24 25   PC/LSCH   10 9 8 7 6 5 4 3 2 1

First Edition

For my troop: Maria, Griffin & Emerson

CONTENTS

A Note About This Story

The tale you are about to read takes place approximately **36.54372 million miles away** from Earth, as the crow flies. It has been collected and woven together via various interview transcripts, recordings, and interstellar **laser screams** sent to Earth from the *Famous Marlowe 280 Interplanetary Exploratory Space Station* over the past decade.

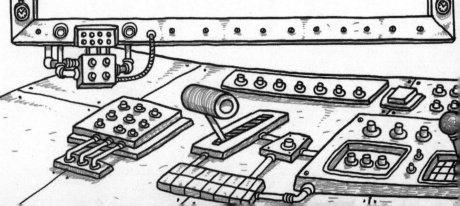

"Laser scream" may be a new term for you, as it is still not well understood on Earth, but we don't have time to get into it here.

The astronauts who boarded the *Marlowe* were charged with **one mission: to discover a planet where humans could one day live**. Captain Isabel Caspian sends out teams of explorers. Finn and his friends are all remarkable, but Finn will always have a special place in the history books.

Because Finn was the first kid born in space.

So in many ways, Finn was born for exactly the type of situation in which we find him here in this book. But it will be up to you to decide if that makes him lucky or not.

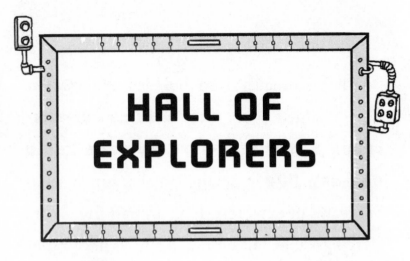

HALL OF EXPLORERS

Abigail Obaro

Troop 301 Captain

Finn Caspian

Chief Detective

Elias
Carreras

Chief Technologist

Vale
Gil

Sergeant-at-Arms

Foggy

Robot

Paige
Caspian

Interloper

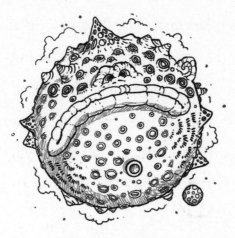

Chapter One
Broken Record

"Okay, guys, I got this," said Vale.

He lifted one arm and pointed a finger at the green sun. Vale Gil was the sergeant-at-arms of Explorers Troop 301. He was responsible for all battle and combat training. (But mostly, he just looked fancy as he fell down.)

He and his friends in the troop traveled all around the universe aboard the *Famous Marlowe*

280 Interplanetary Exploratory Space Station.
Troop 301 had explored many planets.

This had been the most boring one yet.

"Just come on already," said Abigail Obaro.
She was only a month older than Vale, but she
was captain of Troop 301. "I want to finish up
and go home."

"Perfection takes time," said Vale. He held a
rock in his other hand like a quarterback.

"Vale, I thought you said you
wanted to take the lead on this
planet," said Finn. "You said
you were tired of being a
little fiddle?"

"Second fiddle!" said
Vale. "You know the say-
ing is 'second fiddle.'"

Finn laughed. It was easy to get Vale going.
The troop's job was to find a planet where
humans could one day live. And that's what

Abigail and Vale had come to do. That's also what Elias Carreras, the troop's chief technologist, was doing (when he wasn't doodling in his notebook). And that's what Finn Caspian, Troop 301's chief detective, was doing. He and his robot, Foggy, had been taking notes as they walked the strange brown planet.

"This is the one," said Vale.

"Oh, I believe you, Vale!" said Foggy.

Vale didn't really bother to pretend to help. He was most interested in breaking his record. He figured on this low-gravity planet, if he threw a rock as hard as he could, it would go higher than any rock in the history of rock throwing.

"This one is going to set an intergalactic record," said Vale.

He reared back and heaved the stone as high as he could. For a second, it looked like a speck of dust in the green sun's light. When it came crashing back down, Vale jumped in triumph.

"That was a hundred feet in the air, easily," said Vale.

"No way," said Elias. "Maybe twenty."

"You mean a hundred and twenty," said Vale. He turned to Foggy.

"You know I'm right, my robot friend," he said. "That's a new record, right? Mark it for the history books."

Foggy ran a quick calculation.

"Actually, Vale, I measured it and—"

"And it was a record?" asked Vale. "The highest ever?"

"Actually, Elias was—"

"Wrong all along?" asked Vale.

"No," said Foggy. "Please stop interrupting. I was going to say that the rock—"

"Soared like an eagle strapped to a rocket that was late for dinner?" asked Vale.

Foggy looked like he was going to overheat.

"Foggy," said Finn, "he doesn't want you to tell him how high it was. Please just say he's right so we can all move on."

Foggy shook his head.

"But he isn't—"

"Just an incredible rock thrower?" asked Vale. "You're right, Foggy. I'm also a great dancer."

Foggy put his head in his hands. He looked like he might cry.

"You're definitely good at talking too much," said Elias. "Now *shhh* for one second. Do you guys hear that?"

Everyone stopped talking and strained to listen. They had arrived at a patch of long, reedy grass as tall as they were. A soft hiss came from between the blades.

Psssstt.

Someone—or some*thing*—was trying to get their attention.

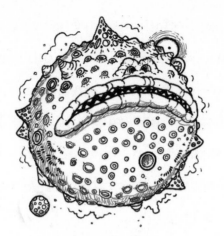

Chapter Two
The Messenger

Abigail put her fingers to her lips.

"Do you want us to stay quiet, Abigail?" asked Foggy.

Pssssstt. The sound came again.

"Yes, that's what she meant," said Finn. "But that doesn't matter anymore."

He pointed at the grass. It started to wave, like something was moving through it.

"Stay behind me," said Vale. "I got this."

Vale was determined to be the hero on this planet. He felt like he hadn't been able to use his training on past missions. And Finn was always getting credit for doing things like stopping planets from exploding. Vale wanted his time in the spotlight.

He reached out and parted the grass.

"Aaaahhh!" he shouted. He leapt back into Foggy's arms. Foggy flew him about ten feet off the ground.

"Are you okay?" asked Foggy. "Were you attacked?"

"I'm fine," said Vale. "But look."

He pointed down at the grass. A large, bug-like creature was poking out its head. It looked like a beetle, but was the size of a beagle.

"Yeesh, I said *pssssstt*," grimaced the beetle. "Don't you know what *psssstt* means?"

No one answered. They were too shocked by this enormous, talking beetle.

"It means keep things quiet, ya know?" said the beetle. "On the qt. The down low. Small ball. Mini talkie."

No one said anything, but Foggy and Vale flew down to the ground to investigate.

"See?" said the bug. "Even that. Too loud. You need to take it down a notch. Inside voices. Whisper misters. Soft vocals. The down low."

"You said that one already," whispered Abigail. "But why do we have to stay so quiet?"

The beetle seemed to laugh at this.

"Duh," it whispered. "So you don't wake up the boss. The big cheese. The head honcho. The top dog."

"And who is that?" whispered Finn.

"Who is the big kahuna?" asked the beetle. "The heavyweight? The muckety-muck and the luckety-luck?"

"Yes," sighed Finn. "Who is that?"

The beetle took another step out of the grass.

Its body was even bigger than they expected. On another day, on another planet, Finn could probably ride it like a pony.

"You're telling me you don't know where you are?" asked the beetle. Everyone shook their heads. "You wanna know who the top banana is? You're standing on her."

The explorers all looked at each other, and then down at the ground. The turf was rough and brown, but it wasn't that strange. They'd been on much weirder planets.

Vale picked up his foot and looked at the bottom of his shoe as if he were checking for dog poop.

"Is she like you?" asked Elias. "Is she a . . . um."

Elias caught himself. The beetle probably

didn't think of itself as a bug.

"A bug?" asked the beetle. "No. Saphrite is not a bug. Saphrite is the planet eater, the colossus, the giant that all giants fear."

"I'm sorry," said Foggy. "Who is this Saphrite?"

"Yeah," said Finn. "And where is she, exactly?"

"Oh, I see," said the beetle. "You really don't know. Bubs, you're not standing on a planet. You're standing on Saphrite. She *is* this planet."

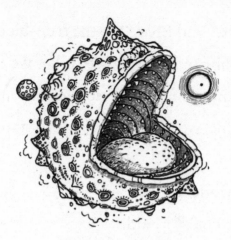

Chapter Three
The Eyes Have It

"I'm sorry," said Foggy. "I believe we're having some language translation problems. You said she *is* the planet. I think you meant to say, she is *on* this planet."

The bug shook its head.

"I'm trying to shoot you straight," it said. "Give you the real deal. The true blue. The no-doubt readout."

"Got it," said Elias. "So the true-blue answer is that Saphrite is the planet? Like, we're standing on an alien so big, so massive, that this whole time we thought we were standing on an entire world?"

The beetle winked.

"True blue," it said.

The kids were stunned. There was nothing in the explorer handbook that could have prepared them for this.

"Okay, I'm calling it," said Abigail. "Game over. Everyone back to the pod."

"Seriously?" said Vale. "We're just going to turn around and leave?"

"This sounds really dangerous," said Finn.

"So Abigail just gets to call it?" shouted Vale.

"It's an alien as big as a planet," replied Finn.

"She's not as big as a planet, she is the planet," said the bug. "She's the whole enchilada. The entire burrito. The complete chimichanga."

"Yeah, but we could make history!" said Vale. "And as sergeant-at-arms of this explorers troop, I say we stay. I'm not scared."

"You jumped into Foggy's arms when the grass made a noise," said Abigail.

"No, I didn't," said Vale. "That was an allergic reaction. But I'm better now. Come on, guys, this is our one chance to really be in the record books. Where's your sense of adventure? Where's the bravery and courage that only a *Marlowe* explorers troop has?"

"I'm with Finn and Abigail," said Elias.

"This bug said Saphrite is a planet eater."

"I did," said the beetle.

"So she literally eats planets?" said Elias.

"Sure does," said the beetle.

"So she'll have no trouble eating four kids and a robot," said Elias.

"She's eaten less accidentally," said the beetle. "And she's not going to be happy that your rock thrower over here woke her up before her alarm."

Vale was about to say it wasn't his fault, but the beetle twitched its antennae.

"Everything you see here is Saphrite," said the bug. "See those majestic purple mountains over there? Those are the spiny ridges of her backbone. And that hill just past the mountains? That's one of her ears."

"So what's this grass?" said Vale.

"That would be her armpit," said the beetle.

"And before you start in on me about how gross that is: Trust me. I know. I'm the jamoke who lives in the armpit."

"Yep, that does it," said Abigail. "Back to the pod. We're getting out of here."

"And that yellow light you see over there?"

said the beetle. "See it, coming up over the horizon?"

"Why, it's a second sun," said Foggy. "How beautiful."

"She'll be glad to hear you say that," said the beetle. "Because that is no sun. That is her eye. And I believe she is looking for you."

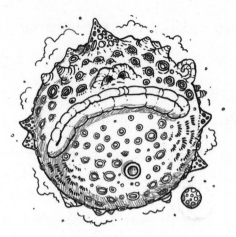

Chapter Four
Open Wide

As Saphrite's eye rose over the horizon, the explorers began to panic. Vale ran toward the grass, Finn and Elias toward the mountains, and Abigail shouted instructions.

"Don't split up!" she yelled. "That never works!"

"A moment, please!" said Foggy. He held

up a hand to slow down the group. "Abigail is right. We must stay together. I believe we should return to the explorer pod."

Finn and Elias turned back to the group.

"Foggy!" called Finn. "Can you please fetch Vale?"

Foggy soared over to the grass and lifted Vale into the air.

"I can see the explorer pod from here," said Foggy. "And I have good news! It is not far!"

"And I have bad news," said Vale. He paused. "Well, there's a lot of bad news, actually."

Foggy flew up higher for a better view.

"It's the *ant*ibodies, isn't it?" said the beetle. "Those jamokes."

"*Ant*ibodies?" asked Abigail.

The beetle explained that Saphrite, like

any other living creature, often gets sick. And like anyone else, when she gets sick, her body produces antibodies. Antibodies are like medicine your body makes to stop an illness in its tracks. For humans, they're little invisible molecules that do battle where you can't see.

"On a giant planet-sized alien like the head honcho here," said the beetle, "the antibodies are actual ants."

A swarm of enormous, purple-armored ants was rushing out of the mountains to the west. They wore purple helmets and waved around thin, sparkling swords. They did not look friendly.

"Yep, we see the ants," said Vale. "And, oops, they're attacking our pod. And—oh no—they are definitely scratching the paint."

"Vale, remember when you said this planet was boring?" Elias said as Foggy and Vale landed. "That was hilarious."

The army of antibody ants spotted the explorers and began marching faster, swinging their swords. The explorers could see another battalion streaming over the opposite horizon, slashing through the armpit jungle. They were coming straight for the *Marlowe* kids. No matter where the explorers turned, they would run into an army of ants.

"The only way we *Marlowe* explorer friends can get out of this situation," said Foggy, "is by going that way."

"Where?" asked Finn.

"There," said Foggy.

The robot pointed at two large hills that were clearly, horrifyingly Saphrite's lips.

"Where now?" asked Abigail.

"Right through there," said Foggy.

"It's so weird," said Elias. "I swear it looks like you're pointing at Saphrite's mouth."

"I am," said Foggy.

"Oh, I get it," said Vale. "You think we should fake like we're running at the mouth. Then we cut back and run to the pod."

"No," said Foggy. "I mean we should go into the mouth."

The explorers were speechless. Foggy was usually so logical. But now he was suggesting they save themselves by being eaten by a giant planet.

"The metal man's got a point," said the beetle. "You're not getting to your ship, and maybe those ants won't follow you down there.

Nobody likes to go down there."

"Why not?" said Elias.

"You'll see," said the beetle.

"Okay, that sounds kinda terrifying," said Finn. "Foggy, what do we do once we get into the mouth?"

"That's when you come up with a new plan and save the day," said Foggy. "It's that simple!"

The antibody ants were now just a football field away from the explorers. The kids could hear them shouting taunts and insults as they got closer.

"Look at those two-legged weirdos!"

"They don't even have antennae!"

"Yeah! And who has only two eyes anymore? That's so nineties."

"Abigail!" said Finn. "It's your call. You're captain."

"I say we stay and fight off the ants!" said Vale. He started swaying his hips. "Come on, it'll be epic! No one will believe us!"

"Vale, what is your deal?" said Elias.

"This is what it's all about!" shouted Vale. "Adventure!"

"Actually, not true," said Abigail. "Right now, it's all about whether we fight off hundreds of armed ants or we dive into a monster's mouth."

"That settles it!" shouted Vale. "History awaits!"

Vale did one of his famous somersault-flip-jump-kick-heel-taps and took off running. He glanced over his shoulder for a second to see how close the ants were, and then ran faster.

Saphrite's eye was now higher in the sky, casting a bright light over the planet.

The explorers ran after Vale. They could see two strange caverns ahead. Vale darted toward them.

"No!" shouted Foggy. "Vale, those are Saphrite's nostrils!"

"Gross!" gagged Vale. He stumbled, turned right, and saw two wide hills. Saphrite's lips.

Elias caught up to Vale.

"I thought you wanted to fight off the ants!" he yelled.

"Nope!" said Vale. "What's more epic than getting swallowed by a giant alien and fighting your way out?"

Elias laughed.

"This is probably your worst idea yet," said Elias. "And I kind of love it."

Foggy flew over them, and Finn and Abigail caught up. They scaled the low hill of Saphrite's bottom lip. But with her mouth closed, there was no way to climb in.

"Okay," said Vale. "I know I've made a lot of mistakes up to this point. I shouldn't have woke Saphrite up."

"True," said Finn.

"And I shouldn't have tried to run away," said Vale.

"It happens," said Elias.

"And I shouldn't have eaten Abigail's freeze-dried candy," said Vale.

"What?!" said Abigail. "When did you do that?!"

"You have to forgive me, Abigail," said Vale. "Group hug."

Vale wrapped his arms around his friends.

"This is getting weird," said Finn.

"And why are we all standing here?" said Abigail. "We have to find a way in or out."

Vale smiled.

"You also have to forgive me for just one last mistake," he said.

He lifted up the boot of his spacesuit. He stomped as hard as he could on Saphrite's bottom lip.

"Yeeeeoooooowwwwww!" bellowed the alien, her mouth opening wide. The sound was like an earthquake mixed with a tornado.

"We're going to be famous!" cried Vale. "Down the hatch!"

Holding on to his friends, he jumped past Saphrite's enormous teeth before the planet could chomp down on them.

Their feet splashed into Saphrite's thick, oozy saliva. And as they sank into the murk, Vale hugged his friends again.

"I wonder what we taste like," he said.

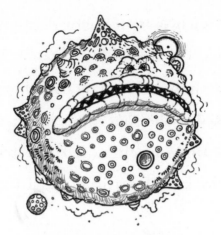

Chapter Five
Slippery Slope

None of the explorers liked to talk about what happened next. Taking a bath in planet-eater spit feels about as good as taking a bath in frog spit. Or crocodile spit. Or hippo spit.

Spit baths are no fun, is the point.

Which is what made Foggy's behavior so strange.

"Um, what is your robot doing, exactly?" said Elias.

A white light beamed up from Foggy's chest and pointed at the roof of Saphrite's mouth. It moved around in a circle, like a searchlight.

"He's looking for a way out, I think," said Finn.

"No, he isn't," said Abigail. "He's doing the backstroke."

It was true. Foggy was floating on his back in the pool of alien saliva. With a kick and a

flutter of his arms, he skimmed from one side of Saphrite's mouth to another.

"It's really fun, isn't it?" asked Foggy.

"Ugh, I'm so jealous," said Vale. "Now Foggy is going to be known as the first explorer to ever backstroke in alien spit."

"What is it with you?" said Finn. "Why are you so obsessed with— Oh no. Oh no, no, no."

Before Finn could finish his thought, he felt something pull at his foot. They all did. Because as Finn spoke, Saphrite decided it was time to swallow them.

Being swallowed by a giant alien was like standing in line for the biggest water slide at the biggest water park in the universe. And then someone pushes you down the slide. And then instead of water on the slide, it's a whole lot of mucus. All you can do is hold your breath and try not to scream.

When they landed in Saphrite's stomach, the explorers looked like they had been dragged through yellow mud. Foggy wiped the muck from the light in his chest and turned it up brighter. The explorers all glanced at each other. Their eyes peeked out of the muck. And they silently agreed they would never speak of this again.

"So, Vale," said Finn. "You know I love you. But maybe someone

else should take the lead?"

"What do you mean?" said Vale. "We're alive because of me. Your sergeant-at-arms has kept you safe this entire time."

"If we ignore the fact that you're the one who awakened Saphrite in the first place," said Foggy.

"Exactly!" said Vale triumphantly. "Foggy gets it."

"Okay, so we need a plan," said Finn. "We went from being on the most boring planet ever to being inside the biggest alien ever. How are we going to get out?"

"I hate to be the one to say it," said Foggy. "Please, excuse me. This is not appropriate. But most life-forms . . . you truly have only two ways out. As far as I know."

"What do you mean?" said Vale.

"Well, there's the way we came in," said Foggy.

"Yeah?" said Vale.

"And then," said Foggy. "Oh, don't make me say it."

"It's okay, Foggy," said Finn. "We're inside Saphrite, but we're also inside a planet. So there has to be more than a couple ways out of here."

"That's right," said Elias. "We need a status report. Foggy, what part of Saphrite are we in?"

Foggy cast his light around the space. It looked like a giant cavern.

"I can tell you," said a voice behind them. It was the beetle.

"Whoa, what are you doing here?" asked Elias.

"Well, truth be told, Saphrite swallowed some friends of mine a couple days ago," said the beetle. "And I want to get them back.

Saphrite had no right to do that. So I thought,
maybe I can help you jamokes, and you can
help me. You know, lend a hand. Loan a foot.
Sign over a tooth or two. You know."

"You are the weirdest bug," said Abigail.

"Okay, so if you're going to help us, what's your name?"

"My name is Jern, but all my friends call me Cool Franky," said the beetle.

"No, they don't," said Vale.

"No, they don't," said Jern. "But I keep trying."

"Well, Jern, it's a pleasure to have you aboard," said Foggy. "Do you have any suggestions for a course of action?"

"Well, you're in Saphrite's first stomach," said Jern. "It's a storage stomach. Really, nothing happens here. We're perfectly safe. Think of this as the lobby. Now we need to get to the prison stomach to save my friends."

"Okay, so how do we do that?" asked Abigail.

"Oh, you want a plan?" said Jern. "A course of action? A direction selection?"

"Yeah," shrugged Abigail. "I mean, I think so?"

"Our plan is to go through each stomach until someone can tell us where the prison stomach is. Then we go there."

"Wait, how many stomachs does Saphrite have?" asked Vale.

"That would be thirty-five," said Jern.

"And how many of them are dangerous?" asked Finn.

"That would be thirty-four," said Jern. "Let's go, team!"

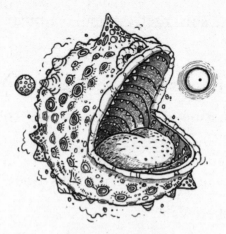

Chapter Six
Grave Situation

Walking from one stomach to another was like exploring a cave system. The rocky, craggy innards of Saphrite narrowed to tunnels that were large enough for the kids to slip through. As they exited Saphrite's first stomach, Vale raced to the front.

"Yeesh, Vale," said Finn as his friend

bumped him. "You don't have to be first every single time."

"When historians write about the time Troop 301 traveled through a giant planet alien," said Vale, "they'll have to start every chapter with me!"

Vale nudged Abigail out of the way and stepped around the beetle.

"Besides, I'm the sergeant-at-arms," said Vale. "I'm the most courageooouuuaaaaAAA-AAHHHHHH!"

Vale had almost stepped off the edge of a cliff. He began flapping his arms like an injured bird. The beetle lunged forward and grabbed his foot before he fell over the side. Vale's screams echoed around an enormous cavern.

The rest of the crew helped pull Vale away from the edge as Foggy shone his light around the giant stomach. The ledge Vale nearly walked off was actually a winding path along the walls of the stomach. Down below, they saw enormous crumbled boulders, huge rock formations, and tall trees tipped on their sides. A valley seemed to dip down into the darkness, where Foggy's light couldn't reach.

"This is the stomach where the planets Saphrite eats are digested," said the beetle. "There are many worlds in here, from across the universe. Digesting a planet is no quick business. It takes a few ticktocks to break down a galaxy."

The troop began making their way along the path. They circled down into the stomach. Every once in a while, they spotted some feature of another world. A dried-up river from one planet, grass from another.

"You jamokes might want to put a little more metal on the pedal," said the beetle.

"Why?" asked Finn.

"Because you're in a stomach, yeesh," said the beetle. "What do you think happens inside stomachs? You think there are couches and sofas and little tea sets for you to drink your little tea?"

"Why is our tea little in this scenario?" asked Finn.

"Well there aren't!" shouted the beetle. "Even if we can't feel it yet, we're all being digested. Broken down. Turned into Her Highness's nutrients. If you want to get out of here alive, you jamokes need to put a little hustle in your muscle."

"I just realized how gross this all is," said Vale.

"You *just* realized that?" shouted Elias. "Come on, let's move."

"That's really something the sergeant-at-arms should say," said Vale.

But the troop ignored Vale, and Abigail pointed out the tunnel to the next stomach up ahead, at the end of the path. As they hurried toward it, Finn spotted a house on one of the crumbled planets. Only half of it was standing, but there was a roof over that half. The front door slowly creaked opened.

But nothing came out.

"That's really weird," said Finn. "Let's just keep—"

"BWAAIINNNSS" shouted a creature with enormous eyes and four arms. It jumped out of the doorway, toward the explorers.

"Zombies!" yelled Vale. "Zombies! We're in a zombie stomach!"

But the tall, thin creature just laughed. It stuffed its four hands into the four pockets of a jacket and leaned against the house.

"Everyone says that," said the alien. The door was about ten feet from the path and about ten feet below it. "At first, I got offended. No one likes to be called a zombie. Then I sort of embraced it. So now I come out of the house and moan 'BWAAIINNNSS.' It passes the time."

The alien trailed off.

"Hi, my name's Finn," said Finn. "We're sorry about the zombie thing."

"It's okay," the alien replied. "Like I said, happens all the time."

"You run into a lot of other . . . visitors . . . down here?" Finn asked.

"There are no visitors," said the alien. "Everyone is either food, or here to stay. I've been here two thousand years already."

"Two thousand years?!" gasped Vale. "I can't stay here that long. I'll miss my eighth birthday party!"

"And eight hundredth," said Elias.

"I'm so sorry," said Abigail, taking control. "It must have been awful to have your world eaten by Saphrite."

"I was pretty sore about it for a thousand years or so," he said. "But I've met so many interesting characters in this stomach. I mean, look at you guys with the bubbles around your heads. Amazing."

"So you know a lot of other creatures living in here?" said Finn.

"Unfortunately, no," said the alien. "They pass through here once and never come back this way."

"Do you happen to know how to get out of here?" asked Vale.

"Sure," said the alien. "You just go through this tunnel and turn right. Then take your second left and you'll see the exit signs. Just follow the sign and head on out. Can't miss it."

"Oh, thank you so much!" said Foggy. "You have been most helpful!"

"Foggy," said Finn. "I think he's joking."

"Of course I am!" said the alien. "I've been here for two thousand years! I have no idea how to get out!"

"Yeesh," said Jern. "What a jamoke."

"Wait a second," said Vale. "You said you're either food or you're stuck here. Do you know anyone else who's been stuck? Our bug buddy here says his friends are locked up in some prison stomach."

The alien thought about it for a minute.

"I don't know where that is," said the alien. "But your best bet is to find a friendly brain and ask it."

"A friendly brain?" said Finn. "How many brains does Saphrite have?"

"Too many for her own good," said the alien. "Or at least more than I have, since I'm still here. If you find a way out, let me know!"

The alien turned around and went back inside his house.

"I don't know," said Vale. "He seemed pretty smart for a zombie."

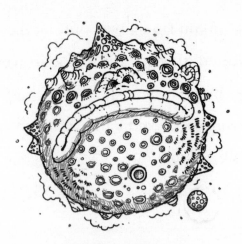

Chapter Seven

So Many Stomachs, So Little Time

The explorers tiptoed out of the planet grave-yard and into another stomach that felt like a cave. A pit of lava bubbled in the center. The explorers all stayed to the edge and slowly moved around it.

"Anyone else not feeling so good?" asked Elias. "My stomach feels kind of funny, and

I'm a little light-headed."

He was walking behind Finn, who was walking behind Foggy. They had almost reached the next tunnel.

"I'm okay," said Finn. "It's probably just the heat. We need to get to the next stomach, and maybe you'll feel better."

The air was cooler in the next stomach and a small pond in the middle made the stomach feel less threatening, but Elias didn't feel better. He said his head hurt and his stomach ached.

"Come on, Elias," said Vale. "You can't say you have a stomachache while you're in an actual stomach."

"*Shhh*," hissed Jern. "Don't disturb the water in that pond."

"Why?" whispered Abigail. "Is there something dangerous in there?"

"I don't know," he said. "But we're in a giant evil alien and there's a weird pond in its fourth stomach. I'd say let's not take our chances."

"Fair enough," said Abigail.

The crew quietly tiptoed out of stomach number four and traveled through three more caverns, narrowly avoiding danger in each one. In the first, a strange purple algae grew and glowed on the walls. They decided not to touch it.

In the next, about a dozen angry mouths rose out of the floor yelling, "Feed me! Feed me!" They decided not to feed them.

And in the one after that, a single fruit grew from a single tree. They decided, no matter how hungry they were, they wouldn't eat it.

"Sheesh, I know I said the outside of Saphrite was boring," said Vale. "But I'm starting to think all her stomachs are going to be boring, too. If we can't do anything, why are we even here?"

"We're here because you thought it would make us famous," said Abigail.

"Oh yeah," said Vale. "I guess I was hoping our epic adventure would be a little more . . . epic."

To get out of the stomach with the tree, they could go left, or they could go right.

"Let's split up!" said Vale. "Jern and I will take one stomach, and you guys take the other."

"I'm not going with the arm sergeant guy," said Jern.

"Sergeant-at-arms!" said Vale. "And why not?!"

"You're trying too hard," said the beetle. "You need to chill out. Cool off. Take a rain drain."

"That doesn't make any sense," said Vale.

"Guys, enough," said Finn. "I think we should stick together. Let's go this way." Finn pointed to the tunnel on the right.

"Fine," said Vale. "We don't have to split up, but at least let me go first."

Finn didn't listen. He was already walking into the next cavern.

"Yeeeoww!" shouted Finn.

"Oooohhh, is something epic happening?" yelled Vale as he ran into the cave.

There was Finn, wrapped in some kind of webbing, hanging from the cave's ceiling.

"Oh man," said Vale. "Why does all the fun stuff happen to Finn?"

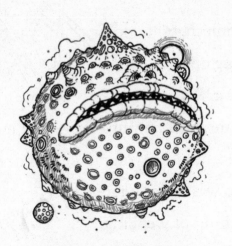

Chapter Eight
Beep Boop

The explorers all clambered into the stomach.
There was Finn, dangling from the ceiling.
And below him was an enormous computer.
Its screen took up one whole wall of the stomach. Lights randomly blinked red, blue, green,
and yellow across the screen.

"Finn, are you okay?" yelled Elias.

"Yeah," said Finn. "Except for the whole

being trapped upside down, hanging from the ceiling thing."

Elias looked closer at Finn. It wasn't a web surrounding him. It was paper. The computer had an enormous reel on one side of it. And the reel constantly spun a thin stream of paper onto the floor.

"Interesting," said Elias, picking up a strip of the paper. "The stomach must have a defense mechanism. It thought Finn was a threat, so it spun him up in a web of this paper."

"Finn, I will be right up," shouted Foggy. He shot off toward the ceiling, but only made it halfway. Like a lasso, the supercomputer whipped paper around Foggy's legs and arms, until the robot was trapped in a paper cocoon.

"Stop," said Jern. "I've heard of this before. Yeah, Saphrite swallowed this one world where everyone would go to play all sorts of games.

A real arcade planetoid. I bet that's where this computer came from."

Elias sat down.

"I'm really not feeling so great," he said.

"Okay, we need to get Elias out of here," said Abigail. "Actually, we need to get all of us out of here. Jern, how do we get Finn and Foggy down?"

"I'm not sure," whispered Jern. "But look. A computer is kind of like a brain. Or a brain is kind of like a computer. And that zombie back at the shack said to look for brains."

"So you think this thing can tell us how to get out of here?" asked Abigail.

"Yeah," smiled Jern. "Or at least how to get to my friends."

The beetle took a confident stride toward the screen.

"Hey, you!" he shouted. "Jamoke! Let go of

our friends and tell us how to get to the prison tummy, wouldja?!"

The computer shot out a small piece of paper. It landed at Abigail's feet. She picked it up and read it out loud.

"It says, 'Where do astronaut computers hang out?'"

"That makes no sense," said Jern.

"Is it a riddle?" said Elias.

"It kind of sounds like a joke," said Abigail.

"But it's only half a joke," said Finn. "Maybe we need to come up with the punchline."

"Oh great," said Vale. "I'm the funny one. I'll solve it."

"We can all solve it together, Vale," said Abigail.

"Yeah, but I'm the sergeant-at-arms," said Vale. "And this is a battle. This is my thing."

"I got it!" said Finn. "Where do astronaut

computers hang out? At the space bar."

A million lights flared on the computer's screen, and bells and horns sounded. Finn had obviously guessed the correct punchline.

Another piece of paper shot out and landed at Abigail's feet.

"Okay, awesome," said Abigail. "This one says, 'What does a robot use to find its keys?'"

"Easy, a flashlight," said Vale. "It needs a light to find the keys, flash drives are . . . like . . . a thing that computers use. Flashlight! Final answer!"

The computer screen lit up entirely in red and buzzed loudly. The paper web around Finn and Foggy tightened. Another piece of paper fell to the ground.

"The answer is: search engine."

"Not as good as mine," mumbled Vale.

"Ow!" said Finn. "Okay, now we know what happens if we get one wrong."

"Don't just shout it out, Vale," said Elias. "We need to work together."

The computer spit out another piece of paper.

"I'll read it," said Vale. He grabbed it before Abigail said anything. "Okay, it says, 'Why couldn't the computer find its home?' I know, I won't answer it. It doesn't even make sense, really—"

"Because it had lost its keys," said Elias. Again, the computer lit up in a rainbow. Bells and chimes filled the cavern.

"That doesn't make sense," said Vale.

"Sure it does," said Elias. "Every keyboard has a home key. The computer couldn't find its home, because it had lost its keys. Its home key. Or maybe not. I don't know. Guys, I'm really dizzy."

"You jamokes need to speed this up," said Jern. "Unless you want the computer to squeeze your friends harder than an aunt at Thanksgiving."

"Okay, fine," said Vale. "I didn't know there was a dad-joke stomach in Saphrite."

The computer buzzed and another piece of paper landed at Abigail's feet. Both she and Vale grabbed it. They began tugging it back and forth.

"Please, guys," said Finn. "Having a little trouble breathing up here! This paper web is really tight."

Vale let go and sulked against the wall.

Abigail read the ticket.

"What do you call four kids, one robot, and a bug, all trapped in an alien stomach?"

"Hmmmm . . . ," said Vale. "It obviously means us, but—"

"I got it!" said Abigail. "What do you call four kids, one robot, and a bug trapped in a stomach? Lunch!"

The computer lit up again, and the paper around Foggy and Finn loosened. Foggy reached over and grasped Finn's shoulder before he fell. The two flew down to the ground together.

"Good one, Abigail," said Finn. "It's kinda dark, but a good one."

"What do you mean?" said Abigail. "Oh. I see now. *We're* Saphrite's lunch."

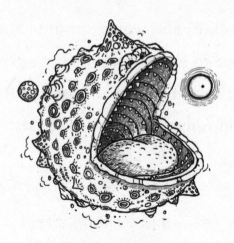

Chapter Nine
Check Out the Big Brain

Each stomach brought a new surprise. They bounced through a rubber stomach, dodged flying meatballs in another, and made friends with little hippopotamus creatures, but refused their offer of tea.

By the time they had moved through at least twenty stomachs, Finn and Elias were almost too weak to walk. Sweat was pouring down

Abigail's face. She wouldn't admit it, but she had started to feel sick, too.

"Jern, how much farther to the prison stomach?" said Abigail. "We need to get there and get out."

"You're telling me," said Jern. "Three of my legs have gone tingly. I think Saphrite is even getting to old Cool Franky."

"No one's calling you Cool Franky, Jern," said Vale, who was the one explorer who didn't feel sick at all. "Come on, guys. Let's just keep going and we'll get there. I know it."

"That's your plan?" said Finn, who was leaning heavily on Foggy.

"Absolutely," said Vale. "It's foolproof!"

After several more stomachs, they turned into a new cave and immediately ran into a big, squishy, squiggly blob.

"Oh, hello," it said as the explorers tried to back out of the room.

"Sorry, sorry," said Abigail as they shuffled back. "Wrong number."

"You must be the little aliens everyone in here is so inflamed over," said the blob.

It didn't move, and they couldn't see any eyes or a mouth on it. But when it spoke, little sparks and lightning bolts seemed to dart across it from side to side.

"I suppose I should sound the alarm, tell everyone you're here. Call down those awful antibody ants."

"No, wait!" said Abigail. "We really need your help."

"My help?" the blob laughed. "No one ever listens to me. I'm just the sixteenth brain. Not good for anything but overseeing Saphrite's toes."

Every time the blob spoke, more electricity shot across it. The explorers could see that it really was a brain—crammed into this smaller

cave like it was forgotten. But its blue, puffy folds definitely looked like the drawings of brains they had seen in books.

"We don't mean any harm to Saphrite," said Finn. "We're just looking for a way out of here."

"This isn't the zoo, dear," said the brain. "You can't just go to security when you get separated from your parents. There's no way out. And if you're getting sick, that just means you're being digested. You won't last much longer."

"No way," said Vale. "We're not food. We'd just end up causing Saphrite heartburn."

The brain seemed to consider this. Tiny lightning bolts flew across the cave, and the explorers all ducked and covered their heads.

"Interesting!" A giant spark shot from one side of the brain to the other, shocking Foggy as he flew up to get a better look. He returned to the ground with the rest of the troop, smoking slightly.

"Do your brains do this, too?" Foggy asked Finn. "I feel all sparkly."

"I don't think our brains are this stormy," whispered Finn.

"I feel tingly, too," said the brain. "I didn't expect my thought to go through you like that. You're different, aren't you?"

"Duh, he's a robot," said Vale. He looked back at his friends. "Some brain on this brain."

"Hmmmmm," said the brain. A quick bolt of electricity shot out and zapped Vale's foot.

"*Yeowch!*" shouted Vale.

"Sorry," said the brain. "Had to check if you were a robot, too."

Finn laughed. He was pretty

sure the brain meant to do that.

"I'm sorry to rush you," said Abigail. "But two of us are feeling sick. And I'm feeling . . . weird. We need to get back home."

"Yes," said the brain. "That will happen in here. It's part of Saphrite's digestion. Feeling ill is just the first stage."

"So I'm being eaten alive?" said Finn. The thought of it made him feel even sicker.

"Yes, all of you are," said the brain. "Except this robot. He seems immune."

"Then why do Finn and I feel sick, and not the others?" said Elias.

"How do I put this?" said the brain. Sparks flew across it as it searched for the right thing to say. "You simply agree with Saphrite. You are easier on her digestion. It is an enormous honor. You should be really proud."

"Oh man," said Vale. "I want to be the one who gets digested."

No one had anything to say about that.

"Please, Your, um, Braininess," said Abigail. "Our friends need to get home. And Jern has been helping us the whole time we've been here. We'd really like to help him rescue his friends. They're in the prison stomach."

The brain's sparks suddenly turned a deep purple and the brain began to buzz.

"Jern, are you a surface creature?" said the brain.

"I am," said Jern. He sounded defiant. Like he was a rebel for living on the surface.

"Ah, then maybe I should throw you in the prison stomach," said the brain. "You know you shouldn't be here."

"My friends were eaten by mistake," said Jern. "They were trying to help Saphrite by guiding a small meteorite into her mouth. And they fell in. It seems only right to free them.

It'll make us even Steven. Square Claire. Balanced Allens."

The brain considered this.

"I'll make a deal with you," said the brain. "I'll tell you which way to go to find an exit. On your way there, you will pass by the prison stomach, but not through it. You'll know when to turn."

The troop sighed with relief.

"But you have to do something for me," said the brain.

"Anything," said Elias. "What do you want us to do?"

"Once you get out, go to Saphrite's right pinky toe," said the brain. "Just below the knuckle, there's an itch that has been driving me crazy for one thousand and three hundred years. Give it a scratch for me."

"That's kind of gross," said Vale.

"We'll do it!" said Abigail, elbowing Vale. "Our sergeant-at-arms will be more than happy to."

A lightning bolt shot out from the brain and shocked Foggy again.

"There," said the brain. "I've put a map of the way out into your robot. It's going to be very dangerous. You're going to have to go straight to the center before you can get out."

A thin line of smoke rose from Foggy's head.

"I'm fine," said Foggy. "But next time, I would pre-fer you use words."

"You must go now," said the brain. "And if you run

into any more brains, please don't tell them I let you go."

The light of the brain's sparks dulled slightly.

"I would never hear the end of it."

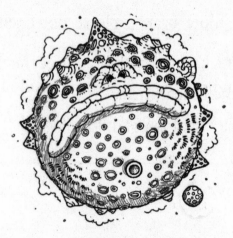

Chapter Ten
A Voice from Above

Foggy led the troop through more tunnels. He was now carrying Finn and Elias under each arm. They were both still awake but exhausted from being slowly digested.

"I can't believe this," said Finn. "Digestion is such a gross way to die."

"Well," said Jern, "you're not *exactly* being

digested. That brain isn't that brainy. Not the sharpest tack in the tack box. Not the brightest bulb in the bulbatorium."

"Please," said Abigail. "Just say it."

"Well, digestion means breaking something down, right?" said Jern. "Decomposing it. That's not what's happening to you. More likely it's the pressure of being inside a giant planet that's getting to you. You're a couple miles underground now. That will do a number on you."

"Not sure that makes me feel better," said Finn.

"Oh, okay," said Jern. "Then yeah, you're being slowly digested by a giant alien."

After shimmying past a gallbladder and bouncing off three different spleens, the troop found themselves in a wide tunnel.

"Chums!" said Foggy. "We are almost

there. It turns out I was wrong about there being only two ways out of Saphrite. You'll be glad to know that Saphrite has a belly button. And when she inhales, a small opening appears in the button. Lucky for us, a small opening on a planet is plenty big for us to squeeze out."

Foggy paused for Vale to make a joke. But

Vale wasn't in the joking mood.

Vale looked at his friends. Finn was nearly asleep. Elias was limp in Foggy's arms. And Abigail looked like she had run a marathon, she was so sweaty.

"Okay," said Vale. "I know I haven't always made the best decisions. But I think I have a plan, and you guys are in no shape to argue." He paused, waiting for them to argue.

"Great," he continued. "Here's how it's going to go down. Foggy, you take Finn, Elias, and Abigail, and you head for that button. Me and the bug are going to bust his buddies out of the hoosegow."

"The what?" said Jern.

"The clink," said Vale. "The big house. The cooler. The crowbar hotel. The stony lonesome. The lonely stonesome."

The beetle looked confused.

"Prison," said Vale. "Once we see it, we'll break them out, and then meet up with my friends on the surface."

"Vale," said Foggy, "I don't think you should be the one—"

"STOP WHERE YOU ARE."

A voice echoed through the tunnel. It seemed to be coming from the walls.

"NO ONE ESCAPES ME."

It was Saphrite. The giant planet had finally taken notice of the explorers.

"Good thing we're not no one," said Vale. "We're Explorers Troop 301, and we always complete our missions."

"YOU MAY NOT THINK I CAN FEEL YOU, BUT I CAN. YOU MAY NOT THINK I CAN HEAR YOU, BUT I CAN. YOU MAY NOT THINK I CAN SEE YOU, BUT I CAN."

"That's . . . really . . . creepy," said Elias. He

was having a hard time staying awake.

"AND I AM NEVER LETTING YOU GO!"

"Why not?" said Abigail. "You're a planet eater. We're nothing to you. Let us go, and we will never bother you again."

"YOU MAY WANT TO ESCAPE . . ."

"Yeah, that's what I just said," said Abigail.

"BUT I WILL NOT LET YOU. MY ANTIBODIES WILL BE UPON YOU SOON, AND YOU WILL HAVE NO CHOICE BUT TO GIVE UP AND BECOME MY LUNCH."

"The lady loves her lunch," said Jern. "You're not going to convince her."

Finn looked around. There was a red light up ahead. He slipped out of Foggy's arms and crawled to the opening. Inside was a small brain. Its bright red sparks flew around its tiny cave.

He turned back around.

"Guys, I don't think that's Saphrite," said Finn. "There's a red brain up ahead. I think it's some sort of alarm system."

"STOP WHERE YOU ARE," Saphrite's voice rang out again. "NO ONE ESCAPES ME."

"See?" said Finn. "It's an alarm. I'd bet you a thousand dollars the next thing Saphrite says is, 'You may not think I can—'"

"YOU MAY NOT THINK I CAN FEEL YOU," said Saphrite at the same time as Finn.

"It's like a recording," said Finn.

"So Saphrite can't actually see or feel us?" said Abigail. "We just tripped a wire? It's all fake?!"

"*Those* jamokes aren't fake," said Jern. He pointed back down the tunnel.

A crowd of angry purple ants were charging toward them. They were hurling insults again.

"Oh look, a couple of them are sleepy. So lazy!"

"Yeah, they're nothing but spoiled food!"

The troop and the bug ran past the alarm brain. A small light shone up ahead, and then went dark again. It blinked on and then darkened.

"That's it," said Abigail. "That's our way out. I know this sounds weird, but I'm so excited to see that monster belly button!"

About twenty feet from the exit, a tunnel opened on the right.

"This is my exit," said Jern "My off-ramp. My fire escape. I gotta go save some jamokes."

"Okay, then I'm coming with you," said Vale.

"No need, friend," said Jern. "I can handle it from here."

"I'm not leaving you," said Vale. He turned

to his friends. "You guys go. Now. You know we have to help Jern after all he did for us. It's the *Marlowe* way. I'm going to help free Cool Franky's buddies."

Jern smiled.

"Vale, you don't have to do this," said Abigail. "Jern can handle himself. We need to get out of here."

"Abigail, please hurry," said Foggy. He had

Finn and Elias draped over his shoulders. "I fear Finn and Elias may not recover if we don't."

"Vale, we're in this together," said Abigail. "Remember, no splitting up. We're a team, always."

"Go," said Vale. "And if I don't make it out, tell everyone on the *Marlowe* what a hero I was."

And with that, Vale turned his back on his friends.

"You called me Cool Franky," said Jern.

"That's right," said Vale. "And you can call me Sergeant-at-Arms Vale Gil."

"Too long," said Jern.

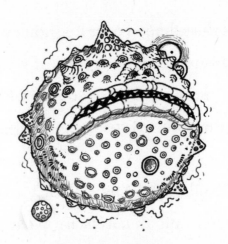

Chapter Eleven
A Hero Is Scorned

Vale watched Abigail dive through Saphrite's belly button. Foggy pushed Finn and Elias through. He turned back to Vale and waved before squeezing himself out.

"Okay, bug," said Vale. "It's you and me. I'll hold off these antibodies while you free your friends. I may not have any weapons. But

I have some sweet karate moves that will make these ants regret ever—"

"Got 'em," said the bug. While Vale had been watching his friends leave without him, Jern had ducked into the prison stomach and broken out *his* friends.

"Wow, that was fast," said Vale. "Are you sure there aren't any more in there? I could help you free them."

"Nope," said the bug. "Turns out stomach prisons aren't all that strong."

Vale was more than a little disappointed. Nothing had gone right this entire adventure. He hadn't set the record for highest toss. He hadn't faced down any enemies in an epic battle. He hadn't solved any of the supercomputer's jokes. And he couldn't even get properly digested!

And now his one opportunity to be a true

hero was gone. He had wanted to defend his new friend while his old friends headed to safety. He had hoped to do some fancy jail-break work, freeing the bug's pals.

At the very least, he wanted to single-handedly defeat an army of ant antibodies.

Well, there was no way that was going to be taken away from him.

"Okay, Franky," said Vale. "There's the exit. You get your friends to safety. I'll hold off these ants."

"That's okay, buddy," said Jern. "We can take them."

Vale shook his head.

"No way," he said. "Your friends are proba-bly weak from being in prison this whole time. Get them to the surface where they belong. This fight is mine."

"Oh, no worries," said Jern. "There were

ninety-seven of them in the prison stomach. So we got this."

"Ninety-seven!" said Vale. "Come on!"

Just then, a swarm of beetles poured into the tunnel. The antibody army stopped dead in its tracks.

"RUN AWAY!"

The ants yelled and scattered into Saphrite's many stomachs and spleens. The fight was over already. And Vale had done nothing.

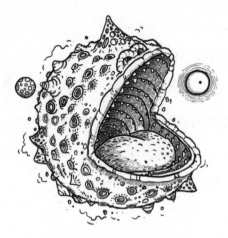

Chapter Twelve
Sergeant-at-Nothing

Vale slunk to the end of the tunnel and poked his head out of Saphrite's belly button.

"Um, Vale?" asked Abigail. "What are you doing?"

"I'm not coming out," said Vale.

Abigail looked around nervously.

"You have to," she said. "We don't have a

lot of time to get to the pod and get out of here. Come on."

"No," said Vale. "This whole planet, I haven't done anything well. I'm supposed to be the sergeant-at-arms, but you guys did everything. Even the bug was more of a hero here than I was."

Finn tried to reason with Vale.

"Come on, buddy," he said. "That's not true. Look, Elias and I are out in the fresh air now and we both feel a thousand times better. It only took a second. You gotta get out of there. Get your head right."

"Yeah, Vale," said Elias. "Come on. You can't stay inside an alien. That's nuts! You've been nuts all day!"

"That's easy for you guys to say," said Vale. "Abigail is the captain, and she's always leading us. Finn is the chief detective, and he solved

those joke clues. Elias is our technologist, and even he guessed one of the computer jokes right. I don't do anything. I need to do something to show how courageous I am."

"Vale, may I?" said Foggy. "I know I'm just a robot, and I don't know much about your squishy human brains. But courage isn't just about fighting and battling."

"Yes, it is," said Vale. "You don't know what you're talking about, Foggy."

"Says the guy with his head sticking out of an alien," laughed Elias.

"My point, Vale, my friend," said Foggy, "is that sometimes the courageous thing to do is *not* to do something. Sometimes the bravest thing you can do is take a step back and let your teammates shine. Trusting your friends like that takes true courage."

"That's such a good point," said Abigail.

"That's why we're a great team," said Elias.

"Your support of all of us makes you a hero," said Finn.

Vale nodded and smiled at his friends.

"Nah," he said.

And he disappeared back inside the belly button.

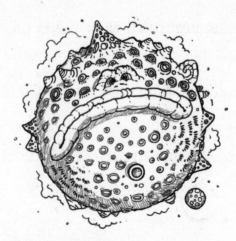

Chapter Thirteen
A Hero's Reception

"Foggy, can you go back in after him, please?"
asked Finn. "Who knows what he's getting up
to in there."

"On it, young Finn," said Foggy. He started
to dive back into the tunnel, when suddenly
Jern burst out onto the surface.

"Jeez, you jamokes sure like to talk," said the

bug. "Flap gums. Chew the fat. Flip the burgers."

"Please, Jern," said Abigail. "Get out of the way."

"Why, you going after Sergeant-at-Arms Vale Gil?" he laughed.

"Yes!" shouted Finn. "Now please move. We need to get in there."

"Sure thing," said the beetle. "But you're not getting back in there anytime soon."

Following the beetle, one at a time, were ninety-seven of his closest friends, all scurrying out to the surface. Ten minutes went by before the stream finally ended.

"Okay, here I go," said Foggy.

"No, wait," said Abigail. "Vale could be anywhere in there by now. If you go in, then we'll have lost two of you."

"What is that jamoke even doing back in there?" said Jern.

"No idea," said Finn. "But Abigail is right. The best thing we can do is get back to the pod and get it ready to fly out of here. We can't stand around and wait for Saphrite to notice us again and send her antibodies. We won't leave without Vale, but let's give him time to get himself out of there first."

The troop ran back to the explorer pod. The antibody ants had done a number on it. The outside was heavily scratched. But there were no cracks in the windshield, and when Abigail powered on the pod, there was no doubt it would be able to take off.

"Let's fly it over to the belly button," said Elias. "So if Vale gets out, we can grab him and go."

"You mean, *when* he gets out," said Finn.

But truth be told, they were all worried.

Abigail launched the pod and flew it toward the tunnel. But before it got even halfway there, an enormous claw rose from the ground. It swatted at the pod, knocking it off course and bouncing it off the hard ground. Or, off Saphrite's hard hide. The explorers looked up to find Saphrite's giant, yellow eye looking right at them.

"She definitely knows we're here," said Abigail.

She pulled up on the levers, but Saphrite's

claw swiped again, knocking the pod back down to the ground where it skidded to a stop.

Abigail tried to lift off again, but Saphrite caught the pod in her paw like a baseball.

"What do we do?" said Abigail. "Every time I try to outmaneuver her, she's quicker than our ship."

BOOM!

Saphrite slammed the pod to the ground, just beside the belly button. The bugs, scared

to be caught up in Saphrite's rage, all scattered.

"Okay, it's okay," said Elias. "Let's just think."

"Yes," said Foggy. "We just need to put our heads together and puzzle this out."

CRACK!

Saphrite began to squeeze the pod, pressing it down into the ground. She was trying to crack the pod open like an egg.

CRACK! CRACKCRACKCRACK!

"That does not sound good," said Finn.

"I don't know how much more of this the ship can take!" said Abigail.

CRACK! WHOOOOOP!

An alarm began to sound on the explorer pod. The ship was going to break open any second.

"Think!" Finn said to himself. "Think. There has to be a way out of this."

"I don't think there is," said Elias.

Suddenly, there was a strange cry from Saphrite's belly button.

"BWWWAAAAAIIIINNNNNSSSS!"

A hand poked out of the belly button. It was followed by an arm, and then another arm. It looked like a zombie climbing out of its grave.

"BWWWAAAAAIIIINNNNNNSSS!!"

came the voice again.

Vale's head poked out of the belly button. And just a second later, he leapt to the surface of the planet. On his back, holding on with all four of his arms, was the alien who had greeted them in the first stomach.

"Hey, guys!" shouted Vale. "I'm back. Thanks for waiting. Remember this guy? The zombie guy? Guess what? Turns out his name is Elav. That's like my name backward. Hey, are you guys okay? You look worried. Were you worried about me? Oh, that's so sweet."

The explorers were all stunned. They couldn't think of a single thing to say, even as Saphrite continued swatting at their ship.

"I'm just kidding," said Vale. "I know you're really worried about the

pod. One sec. Elav, give me a hand?"

Vale and the thin alien ran toward Saphrite's paw.

"Vale, no!" shouted Abigail. Saphrite swung at Vale.

"Triple-dip-flip!" yelled Vale, and he jumped, soaring between the claws and then flipping so he could grab on to a giant knuckle. Elav pulled off the same gymnastic stunt.

"Here," said Vale, pointing at a spot on Saphrite's paw. Vale used his two hands, and Elav his four hands, to scratch the thousand-year itch on Saphrite's toe.

"This one's for you, sixteenth brain," said Vale.

Saphrite was so relieved, she closed her massive yellow eye. She lay her paw on the ground. And that rumble across her mountains just might have been a purr.

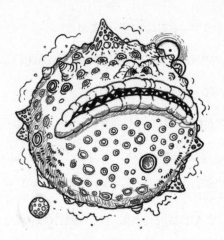

Chapter Fourteen
History in the Making

On the long ride back to the *Marlowe*, the explorer pod shook and shuddered. Saphrite had definitely done some damage. But the ship would make it. The explorers would make it. And they would have one great story to tell.

Elav was along for the ride. He didn't have a home planet anymore, but the kids couldn't just leave him on Saphrite. So they agreed to drop him off at their next stop.

"Vale, you're out of your mind," said Finn. "What were you thinking?"

"I'm sorry, guys," said Vale. "I don't know why I got so obsessed with being the hero of this trip. It's just that you guys all have these really cool things you do. And, you know, I want to be able to say I do cool things, too."

Abigail shook her head.

"Vale, you're helping us all the time," she said. "Just because you don't always defeat the big bad guy doesn't mean you're not a hero."

"I know that now," shrugged Vale. "What Foggy said really hit me. All his talk about being part of the team. I know it probably looked like I wasn't listening. And you probably thought I went back in to be a hero."

"It did look like that," said Elias, "because you said, 'Nah,' and ran off."

"True blue," laughed Vale. "But what you

guys were saying about being a team really hit me. And it made me think of old Elav over there. He was all alone in that half-a-house. And he'd been that way for two thousand years!"

Vale paused to look over at the four-armed alien.

"I just couldn't imagine that," he said. "And I felt like we couldn't leave him behind."

"That's really sweet, Vale," said Finn. "We should write this whole story down. They can teach it to future explorer troops. How Vale Gil risked his own life—"

"And the lives of his friends," laughed Abigail.

"How Vale Gil risked everything," said Finn, "to save just one alien who was alone in the universe. That would make an amazing story."

"Nah, that's okay," said Vale. "I don't care about that stuff anymore."

"Really?!" said Elias. "I don't believe you."

"Really," said Vale. He put his arms behind his head and closed his eyes. "I don't need all that fame stuff. I'm a legend in my own mind."

The troop all laughed.

"We'll definitely tell everyone how you got covered in Saphrite's mucus," said Abigail.

"You can leave that part out," said Vale.

"Or how you made best friends with an armpit beetle," said Elias.

"How dare you speak of Cool Franky like that!" shouted Vale.

"Oh yeah, and we'll definitely tell everyone about how you scratched Saphrite's itchy, flaky, gross toe," said Finn.

Vale's eyes opened, and he shuddered as a chill ran down his spine.

"Never," he said.

"Yeah, I think you still have some flakes on your forehead," laughed Abigail.

"Eww!" cried Vale. "Get them off!" He slapped at his forehead, but there was nothing there. All his friends were laughing so hard, the little explorer pod shook.

"Very funny," said Vale. "We shall never speak of the toe again."

THE *FAMOUS MARLOWE 280* INTERPLANETARY EXPLORATORY SPACE STATION

HALL OF ALIEN STOMACHS

DESPITE TRAVELING THROUGH AN IMPRESSIVE AND DISGUSTING ARRAY OF STOMACHS, EXPLORERS TROOP 301 ONLY SAW A HANDFUL OF SAPHRITE'S MANY DIGESTIVE CAVES.

HERE ARE SOME OF HER MORE FAMOUS TUMMIES.

THE COMET CHAMELEON

Saphrite has been known to pluck a comet out of the starry sky and pop it in her mouth. Once

in her stomach, the com-
ets, with their long tails
and changing colors,
resemble sleeping lizards.

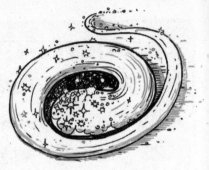

They've been known to crawl out of the comet
stomach and into other lairs, blending in with
their surroundings.

THE BALLOON BALLROOM

The explorers were lucky not to encounter any
of Saphrite's many bladders. They fill with all
manner of fluids. What fluids, you ask? Do not
ask such questions. You do not want to know.

HAMSTER WHEEL

It's just a big hamster. In a giant wheel. Running. No one is sure what the hamster wheel is powering, but one thing is for sure: the hamster is in great shape.

STARBELLY

Saphrite loves to eat planets, but all those crusts can give her indigestion. When she needs to do a cleanse, she swallows a couple young stars to help settle her stomach.★

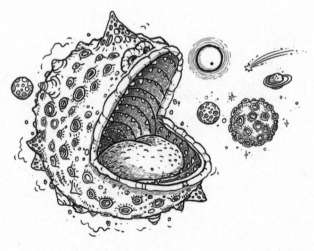

*Eating stars is not FDA approved and is not guaranteed to improve your digestion. Consult with your doctor before eating a star. If you've eaten a star and feel gassy, call your doctor. Side effects may include glowing skin, fire breath, and explosion.

Acknowledgments

When I first got started as a writer, I made a huge mistake: I wrote for grown-ups. But, as we all know, grown-ups are boring. And they make very serious faces when they read. And they read books with titles like *The History of How Wallpaper Makes Me Feel*. And do you know what grown-ups like to do when reading at night? Fall asleep!

Ridiculous.

I have since sworn off adults and I've never been happier. So I'd like to thank every kid who has ever listened to the Finn podcast or read one of these books. The kids I have met through the Finn universe have made my world infinitely brighter and I can't thank you enough.

Now, having said that, maybe a grown-up is

reading this to you now. Or maybe they bought this for you. Or maybe they helped you check it out from the library. That makes this a little awkward. But please put on a very serious face and tell them I'm sorry I called them boring. And then thank them. Stories are incredible gifts, and the people who bring them to us are very special.

So I would like to thank a very special person to me: my mother, Susan, who always encouraged me to read. Thank you for pretending not to see the flashlight beam under my covers as I stayed up way past my bedtime reading late into the night.